The Three Billy Goats Fluff

For pom-poms, peg dolls, and peppermint creams!
For my dear grandparents.
And for Holly and Daisy, who would have loved them too. R.M.xx

To
Molly and Joe
L. P. x

tiger tales

an imprint of ME Media, LLC
5 River Road, Suite 128, Wilton, CT 06897
This paperback edition published in the United States 2013
First published in the United States 2011 by tiger tales
Originally published in Great Britain 2010
by Hodder Children's Books
a division of Hachette Children's Books
Text copyright © 2010 Rachael Mortimer
Illustrations copyright © 2010 Liz Pichon
CIP data is available
Hardcover ISBN-13: 978-1-58925-101-4
Hardcover ISBN-10: 1-58925-101-6
Paperback ISBN-13: 978-1-58925-439-8
Paperback ISBN-10: 1-58925-439-2
Printed in China
WKT0612

For more insight and activities,
visit us at www.tigertalesbooks.com

The Three Billy Goats Fluff

by RACHAEL MORTIMER

Illustrated by LIZ PICHON

tiger tales

Trip-trap

Trip-trap

How was
he supposed
to sleep?
Mr. Troll buried
his head in his pillow
and groaned.

He looked back at the newspaper advertisement:

How could he have fallen for it?
What the advertisement had NOT said was:

WHOLE HOUSE AVAILABLE

NOISY!
UNDERNEATH THE ONLY BRIDGE FROM THE ROCKY MOUNTAIN TO THE LUSH GREEN FIELD.

A ROOM WITH A TRASHY VIEW

On the mountain next to Mr. Troll's bridge lived the three Billy Goats Fluff. They loved to eat the lush green grass in the field by the bridge. It made their fleeces extra fluffy, important for Mother Goat's knitting business.

FLUFFY
STUFF
FOR
SALE

The three Billy Goats Fluff crossed the bridge twice a day.

But this morning, Mr. Troll had a surprise for them. He'd put up a sign:

Little Billy Goat Fluff had not yet learned to read, so he set off as usual. He'd just put one hoof on the bridge when Mr. Troll leaped out!

"I'm a Troll with
a very sore head.
Stop trip-trapping
over my bed!
When I'm tired and feeling blue,
there's nothing quite like
little goat stew!"

Little Billy Goat was very scared
and scampered back to Mother Goat.

Next came Middle-sized Billy Goat Fluff. His hooves were louder than Little Billy Goat's. Mr. Troll leaped out again!

"I'm a Troll
in a very
bad mood.

Waking me up
is terribly rude!
Middle-sized goat makes
a lovely roast.
Or tasty pâté upon
my toast!"

Middle-sized Billy Goat
raced back to Big Billy
Goat. They were both too
scared to cross the bridge.

"We're telling our mom on you!" they shouted.

Mother Goat listened to her Billy Goats and she thought about Mr. Troll. She knew what it was like to live without sleep; Little Billy Goat woke her up every night!

Once upon a time...

SUPER GOAT!

BIG BILLY Goat

Middle Billy Goat

Little Billy Goat

That night, as she sat knitting booties from the finest billy goat fluff, Mother Goat had an idea….

The next day, Mr. Troll was waiting for them!

"I'm a Troll who's really cross.
It's time to show you I'm the boss!
When I'm tired, I need to eat
goat and fries! My favorite treat!"

Big Billy Goat trembled as he handed Mr. Troll a present and note from Mother Goat.

If you can hear us trip-trap by,
then you can make three Billy Goat pie.
But if we're quiet as tiny mice,
You must stop being grumpy and
start being nice.

Little Billy Goat Fluff was the first to try out Mother Goat's plan. He shakily put on the hand-knitted booties. They were so fluffy. Bright yellow. His favorite color!

Slowly, he stepped out onto the bridge. Mr. Troll listened from his bedroom. Nothing? Nothing!

Middle-sized Billy Goat Fluff was next. His hooves were quaking as he put on four exceedingly fluffy booties.

Pink! Middle-sized Billy Goat was a real softie.

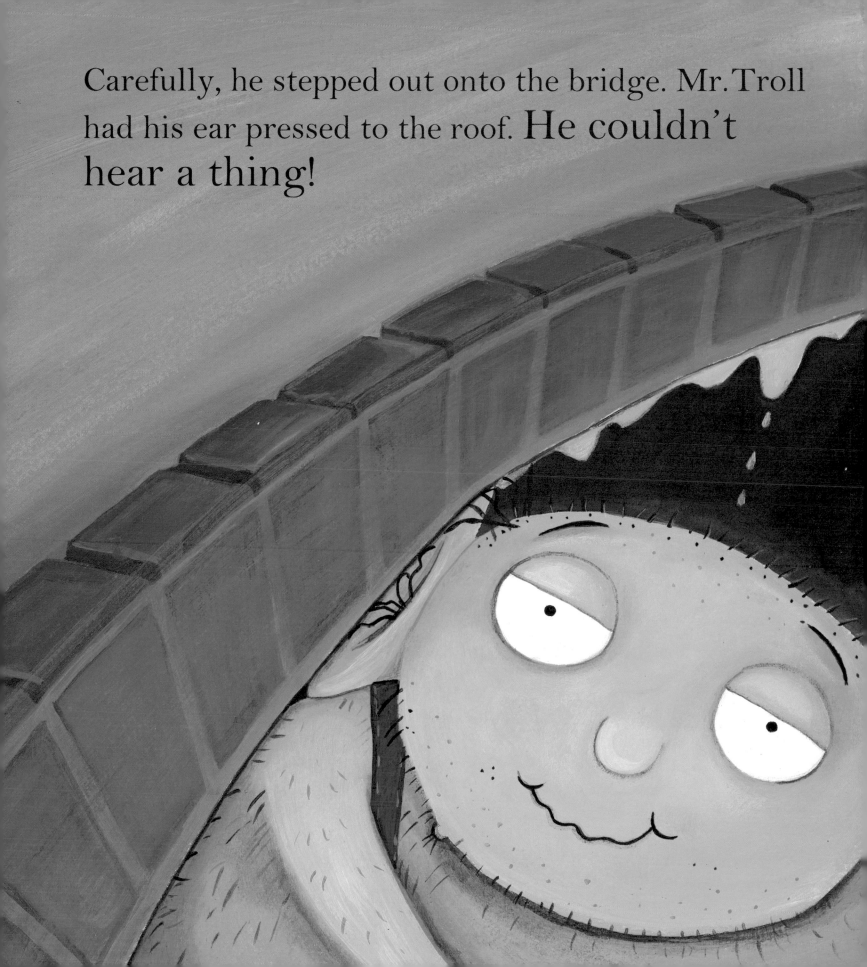

Carefully, he stepped out onto the bridge. Mr. Troll had his ear pressed to the roof. He couldn't hear a thing!

Finally, it was Big Billy Goat Fluff's turn. His booties had taken most of the night to knit. With four huge pom-poms on his hooves, Big Billy Goat stepped onto the bridge.

Mr. Troll strained his ears.
Silence, at last!
How had they
done it?

Mr. Troll came out from under the bridge. He looked at the three Billy Goats Fluff happily munching the grass in the field. He looked at his present from Mother Goat. Then he opened it.

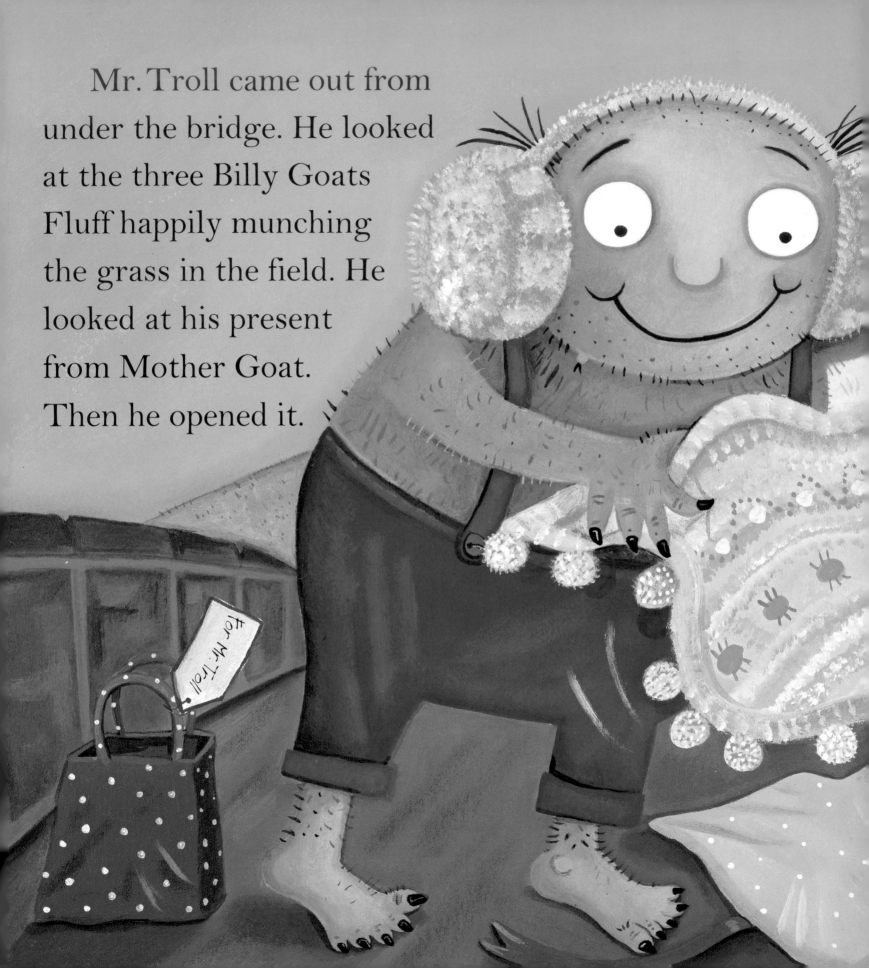

Inside were the fluffiest earmuffs he had ever seen, wrapped inside one of Mother Goat's special blankets.

Dear Mr. Troll,
We are very sorry for waking you up. We hope this gift helps you have your best sleep ever.

Love,
Mother Goat and
the three Billy Goats Fluff

That night, Mr. Troll drank a hot mug of beetle juice.

TROLL'S MUG

FAIRY TALES FOR TROLLS

He read his favorite
bedtime story.

The Princess and the Troll

Troll

Then he put on his big fluffy earmuffs
and cuddled his soft green blanket.

For the first time in his new house, he slept and slept. He dreamed of fluffy clouds, fluffy toads, fluffy beetle juice, and best of all, his new quiet friends . . .

the three Billy Goats Fluff!